BORN A WITCH...
DRAFTED BY THE FBI

BOOK 0 IN THE FEDERAL WITCH SERIES

TS PAUL

GREAT GO   UBLISHING

DEDICATIONS

Special thanks to Michael and to my wife Heather who keeps me grounded and to Merlin the Cat, we are his minions.

CHAPTER ONE

"I INSIST that you do something about that child!" Camilla Blackmore was a mean-spirited woman. She was on her fourth husband. Number three dropped dead at the grocery store surrounded by innocent people. If she were killing her husbands, they were the perfect murders.

"What has Aggy done now?"

"What hasn't she done! That child is menace! Have you noticed the squirrels lately? Whatever she did to them was on a genetic level. They are breeding like that. Changing nature is against the rules, Marcella. You, yourself, should know that."

"Camilla, calm yourself. She transmuted the squirrels when she was barely four years old. She holds the record for the youngest witch to perform a transmutation." Marcella Blackmore was the oldest and current matriarch of the Blackmore clan. She was also the High Priestess of the Clan.

"Why do we celebrate this? She didn't zap just one squirrel. She zapped all of them for ten square miles! Purple! She made the squirrels purple. They have become a tourist attraction for the Goddess's sake. I have to chase mundanes off my lawn every morning. For some reason, my yard attracts the little monsters."

"The tourists or the squirrels?" Camilla made a nasty face at Marcella.

"The squirrels of course! The mundanes are just annoying. I would zap those lavender tree rats, but they are immune to magic!"

"The money those tourists bring into our shops has been good for the family. You can't discount that."

"Fine. Whatever. Her mistake as a young child can be forgiven. It is all the other things that we cannot forgive."

"Camilla, seriously? We all make mistakes when we come into our power. Even you did crazy things. I can remember making Mother's clothes three sizes smaller so they would fit me. I can still feel the sting of Father's belt to this day. A brave man, my father."

"I remember making all the bushes on the property taller, not changing the genetic makeup of animals." The two women were standing on the back porch of the Blackmore mansion. The backyard was a jungle of herbs and flowers. The perfect place for a young witch to get lost in. I could hear them, but I was essentially hidden from view.

"It was just some squirrels, Camilla. She will do great things one day. You know she will. Our seer has foretold she will change the world."

"That is if she doesn't kill all of us first. Her magic is out of control. The simplest things go haywire, and chaos happens. Her change could be permanent. I have no intention of living out my life as a pink chicken or some other creature. Her poor mother."

Marcella's face got very stern, and she glared at Camilla. "That was not the child's fault, and you know it. Teegan's mental collapse was more the fault of losing her husband than it was Aggy's misadventure. That was just a coincidence. That party was too much for her that day."

Camilla blew out a breath. "My ass! What was it? Her seventh birthday? I was there Marcella. My dear husband and I organized the damn thing. I was the one who invited the other children. You cannot change my memories of the incident."

I bowed my head at the mention of Mommy. It wasn't my fault. It really wasn't. Poor Daddy had died the year before on my sixth birthday. He was bringing a cake back from the store when a drunk driver hit him, and he died. I felt a tear roll down my face. Pulling out my handkerchief, I wiped my face. Mommy cried for almost a year. She was finally almost back to normal when the incident happened.

"Then the blame for the incident is on your head, Camilla. Yours and Harrison's. Teegan was not ready for guests, much less a yard full of young children. And then there were the gifts. Really, gifting a young child a Unicorn? She was far too young for that."

"Don't blame Harrison, may he rest in peace. He thought she would like a Unicorn. What witch child hasn't dreamed of riding one? I know that Teegan and I both wanted one as children. It's a status symbol, that's all. Only witches ride in style."

Marcella shook her head. "Agatha apparently. Camilla, I don't know why you are blaming her. Only the Unicorn was affected. None of the other children had so much of a hair harmed on them. You should know that we ran diagnostic spells immediately after the event."

"It was the shock of it. Poor Teegan. She fainted dead away. After that she was never quite right. I visit her, you know. Every week I check on her progress at St Bridget's."

"It was not Aggy's fault, and you know it. If Teegan had been more aware, she would have noticed the strength of her child's magic. Teegan was never as strong a witch as you are Camilla. She wasn't ready to accept that her daughter was so strong at such an early age. I myself would be very hard pressed to whip off a spell such as that without any preparation."

"Once again, my whole point Marcella. She zapped that poor creature right in front of everyone! Then she tried to fix it and only made it worse. Has anyone been able to fix it?"

Marcella winced again. She breathed out a huge sigh. "No, we have not. It's not for lack of trying, mind you. I have had every traveling witch or wizard come and take a look. I even sent to Europe for one of their dispelling mechanics. Nothing. She did something... They all say the same thing. It was an impossible spell. Especially for a seven year old."

"Have you considered what would happen if she does it again? It might be a person this time. She is a walking time bomb."

"So, in your opinion, we should parade the child around like a broken toy and subject her to the ridicule of the mundanes? Is that what you are saying?"

"That is not what I am saying at all! You are putting words in my mouth now. She is seventeen years old. It's not like we can just send her off to college with the rest of the children her age. Won't any of the witch schools take her?"

"You know the answer to that one since it is your fault they won't even consider her." The older woman had a cross look on her face.

The younger woman hung her head in shame. "For that I am sorry. At the time, I was frightened for my own daughter. Winter could have been harmed, and I was very upset. She is the one bright light in my life. I just could not allow Teegan's daughter to attend any school Winter attended." Marcella rolled her eyes at the bright light comment.

"So nice of you to worry about your daughter and screw over your sister's daughter, your niece, at the same time." Marcella's voice was so cold her breath could have frozen water.

"How many times must I say that I am sorry for that? Grandmother, I was scared."

Marcella shook her head. "That was not an excuse then, and it still isn't one now. You are a full-grown witch with mastery of your powers. Being afraid of a mere child does not make the coven or the clan look good in the eyes of the council. You are *this close* to being censured." She held up her hand in a pinch.

"Me? They want to censure me? How dare they! Why haven't they done anything about her?" She pointed toward the garden.

4

"What makes you think they haven't? Aggy has had the best homeschooling teachers that money could buy. She just needs some refining and a purpose to her life. Come inside and I will explain." Marcella pushed Camilla toward the doors. She looked over her shoulder and caught my eye. There was no hiding from her. She shook her head at me.

"Why do you care so much about what that old bat of a witch thinks? She just wants to ship you off to some boarding school or something."

"Who, Grandmother or Camilla?" I glanced back at the house. They had gone back inside. I went back to picking flowers. Grandmother promised to show me how to weave them into a crown. Tonight was midsummer.

"Camilla of course. That bat has it out for you. She has ever since your birthday party."

"Fergus, you aren't still mad at me because of that are you? I can try to fix you again if you like."

"No! Don't. I really don't want to get smaller or turn into one of those squirrels this time. I would look terrible in purple. No offense Agatha, but your magic can be a little lopsided in its effects."

"Lopsided. I have never thought of it like that. Remind me to tell Grandmother the term. The squirrels were a mistake. I was only four years old. I can do the basics without bad things happening." I pointed at the flowers I just picked and muttered 'danzleikr.' The flowers sat up and began to dance. The held each other's leaves and danced around me. I spoke 'stǫðva.' They all collapsed on the ground and lay still. I scooped them up and placed them in the basket by my feet.

"Things like that I can do. It's when I try big spells or off-the-cuff things that disaster happens. Like at the party. All the girls were screaming and the parents were freaking out. I reached for

Momma and she was on the ground. I just reacted and tried to reverse it."

"Tell me about it." Fergus was my sort of familiar. He was a unicorn.

"Let's take these into the house. Maybe Aunt Camilla is gone."

"Do you want me to stab her? I can get her good. Once you go horn, you never go back!"

I looked down at Fergus. He was shaking his head and dancing about like he was fighting someone. I could only shake my head and laugh. Unicorns! It's all about the horn with them.

"Don't make her mad. She is still a little scared of you. Don't remind her that she is the one that paid for you in the first place."

"Like she could take me back now. It's been what, ten years? Who would buy a used micro unicorn?"

I braced myself and stood up. Careful not to step on my friend, I scooped up the basket and started to walk toward the house.

"Hey! Super short Unicorn here! Did you forget about me?"

I reached down and scooped my little friend up. He was pocket sized. I have special pockets on all my shirts made just for him. They are lined with spell-infused Kevlar. He gets a bit pointy sometimes.

"Oooh, I get to ride on the boob again!" He began jumping about in my hand.

I held him up to eye level. "Cut that crap out, Fergus! I'm sure Zeus would give you a ride back to the house. How about I give him a call?"

"I'll be good! I promise. Just keep that monster away from me." The tiny Unicorn shuddered at the thought of being Zeus's plaything again.

"He's not that bad, Fergus. You know he won't eat you or anything. He just wants to play."

"Yeah, fun."

I smiled to myself. Threatening Fergus with Zeus was one of my standard threats that worked with the little terrorist. Zeus was my Grandmother's familiar. He was a what is known as a Savannah cat.

He was a hybrid of a Serval cat crossed with a Siamese cat. He was big, really big, and Fergus was his favorite toy.

I could still hear voices inside the house as I climbed the stairs to the wrap-around porch. The mansion was an early Victorian showpiece. Three stories with a wrap-around porch, it has been used as a model for several Hollywood movies. Every time she sees one of those movies, Grandmother calls her lawyer and sues them. Magic Margaritas, indeed.

I sat down in one of the really comfy wicker chairs that lined the back porch. I had lived here since my seventh birthday. This house had so much history in it.

Grandmother liked to tell the story of how the house was originally constructed to serve as a hotel for the town. Her father had other ideas and had hexed the owners into selling it to him for less money than it cost to build. The town elders had, of course, been outraged that he would dare to impose his will upon others in such a way. He got away with it by saying that a hotel would only attract strangers to town and expose all of us. Thus, our clan gained a house and the town a new alderman. He never wanted to be mayor. He was content to stay in obscurity.

Supernaturals came out to the world twenty years later. Germany declared war on Europe in a mad power grab and made use of its Adepts and witch covens. We, as a people, were dragged into the light. The mundanes didn't know what to believe. Magic was real. So were the mythological creatures that made things go bump in the night. The Huns were using vampires, backed up by witches, to kill Allied soldiers in the dark of night all across Europe. The Allied powers were desperate, and patriotic paranormals volunteered for service by the dozens. Grandmother said that their reasoning was this: "Join now, and be seen as heroes. Hide and don't help, and be persecuted for it later."

For many, neither was a good choice. The Vampires suffered the most of all the paranormals. The British army was getting annihilated on the Western front and they were desperate. They made a deal with the witch and wizard councils. If they took care of the Vampire threat, the government would formally recognize the paranormals and incorporate them into the country. Someone knew the proper cheese to use when luring rats. They of course leapt at the offer. A great spell was created. British vampires, in a rush to be patriotic and avoid future persecution, even volunteered to help. The nests here in America told them it was a bad idea and pleaded with their brethren to avoid the battlefields.

The great spell was triggered on Valentine's Day. The covens claimed it was to harvest the energy of love to bring about change. Stupid mundanes fell for it. If they had been paying attention, they might have noticed that it was actually Lupercalia they were celebrating, not a holiday named after a Christian saint. It was a festival of sacrifice and that is what they did. They sacrificed the leader of the British Nests in a symbolic blood sacrifice. He was supposed to survive. He didn't. Neither did any vampire within five thousand miles of Paris, France. As a race, they were devastated. Only those on the West coast of North America and those in Asia survived what became known as the Great Purge. Needless to say, the Huns were defeated. In the aftermath, laws were enacted to give all paranormals the same rights as norms. Or at least that is the theory.

I heard a door slam and tires screech away. It looked like Camilla had left. I stood up and stepped into the house.

"Grandmother? Are you still here?" She wasn't in the kitchen or the still-room. Those were her favorite places to relax after a visit from one of the more strident family members.

The parlor was filled with really uncomfortable Victorian era furniture that she claimed her parents bought. It was only used for special occasions. I knew she wouldn't be in there but I looked, anyway. "Grandmother?"

The front room was where many coven meetings were held if the weather didn't cooperate. She wasn't there either. I raised my voice. "Grandmother? Are you here?" I was starting to get worried.

"In here, child." I blew out a breath in relief. Camilla could be a handful, but she only killed husbands, or at least that was the family rumor.

Grandmother was sitting behind the massive oak partners desk in her office. I loved that desk. It had to weigh a good five or six hundred pounds. The backside was covered in drawers. As a child I liked to peek in them looking for sweets or things to play with. The top of the desk was covered in really cool green stained leather that she said was original to the desk.

"Are you OK Grandmother?" She smiled at me and closed the folder in front of her. I caught a glimpse of some sort of government seal as the file closed.

"I'm fine, Aggy. Have a seat, please." She clasped her hands together in front of her. As I watched, she studied them for a moment and rubbed them together. "I guess you heard Camilla voice her concerns and comments?"

From my pocket the muffled voice of Fergus could be heard saying. "Yeah, we heard the old bat! You should tell her to go kiss a warthog and leave us alone." I giggled and pulled him out of my pocket. He stood on the desk and began walking back and forth as if pacing.

"I won't apologize for her to you, Aggy. She is family."

There was one rule. Family is everything. We didn't hurt family.

"I understand. Are you sending me away like she asked you too?"

The older woman shook her head. "Heard that did you? Well I need to do something with you, my dear. I have taught you almost everything that I know. Regardless of what my daughters will say, you are my best student and will be my successor one day."

I started to protest, but she held up her hands to stop me. "Hear me out Agatha, please."

"I will listen."

"Thank you. Ignore Camilla and the rest of them. They know very little of the training you have had. You have all of my knowledge in herbs, lore, and practicality. They never chose to learn any of that. The members of our coven have been exposed to too much television and Hollywood theater. Power and magic is not the solution to everything. You must use your head and your heart to show you the way. None of them have shown any interest in learning. They believe that my successor is Matrilineal. The council, of course, knows better. Believe it or not, none of them have ever asked. Your mother... She may have been a victim of someone who broke the first rule. It is one of the reasons I have kept you here rather than allow you to go to one of the schools."

"I thought that they wouldn't take me because of Camilla?"

"Trust me. If I asked, they would have taken Fergus as a student. Camilla is too easy to guilt."

I started laughing. My Grandmother was very sharp.

She let me calm down, then looked at me seriously. "Now, we have much to discuss. You need to receive training, but it doesn't necessarily have to be from the witch schools. Have you thought what you want to do with your life? Do not say run a shop in town, because I know you better than you think I do."

I thought hard about it. I knew what I wanted to do deep in my heart, but it was something regarded with contempt by almost every paranormal race.

"Spit it out Agatha. I won't be offended."

I looked down at Fergus and he had a look in his eye directing me to tell her the truth. "I want to join the police and help people." I half expected her to yell at me. I looked up, and she was smiling.

"Very good. Did you think I would miss all the mysteries and crime books you read? Or the cops and robbers show you like on the idiot box? Child, I pay very close attention to what interests you. Now, down to business. What exactly do you want to do? Do you want to work with Cappy and be his new deputy or strive for something bigger?"

Cappy was the police chief here in our little slice of heaven called Blackbriar Heights. He cruised about town in an old police cruiser that has seen better days. His primary function was to keep the mundanes out of trouble.

"Bigger. No offense Grandmother, but we don't have crime here."

"We do, but you would not have heard about it. No, I will not explain. You can ask me later after you finish school."

"What school am I going to?"

"How about the FBI Academy? Would you like to work for the US Government?"

"Really? How?"

"The Council has been trying to get someone to join for a few years. The Feds have to deal with paranormal crime on a daily basis. Some of the less powerful groups already have trained agents serving. They have been asking for a magic user for a while."

"And they want me? Don't they know about the mistakes and bad stuff that happens?"

"Dear one, even the Council knows that it is not your fault. They have offered to train you, under the auspices of the FBI, of course. If you want to help people, this is your chance."

I, of course, said yes. So begins my journey. Wish me luck because heaven help the FBI if I cut loose. I hope they have good insurance.

CHAPTER TWO

My first day at my new school was a disaster. Once again, not my fault in the least. This time I'm blaming Fergus. Let me back up a week or so.

A week after Midsummer's Eve, Grandmother had a visitor. I was out in the garden as usual when I heard a car pull up out front. A few moments later, my Grandmother called to me from the house to come inside. I carefully placed the sumac and mandrake root in my basket, being vigilant to separate the two. Our herb garden is extremely large. Grandmother meticulously keeps the really scary poisonous plants separated from the rest. No point in accidentally poisoning the coven members. Personally, if they don't know their herb lore. it serves them right to get sick. I took off my protective gloves and grabbed the basket. Just as I was about to close the gate to the segregated area, I heard a voice from the lavender patch.

"Hey! Don't leave me out here alone!"

Peering into the patch, I saw Fergus standing on a rock. "I thought you wanted to keep playing with the field mice?"

"More like tag. They have no sense of fun. I'm just trying to show them a good time, that's all. Promise!"

I rolled my eyes. "I think they understand what your idea of fun is by now. If you're coming, get over here!"

Unicorns! Horniest creatures on the planet. Grandmother tells me all the time that Satyr's are the worst, but I've not met one of those yet.

Fergus galloped over to the path and stood at my feet. I scooped him up and tossed him into the basket.

"Hey! What the freaking hell!"

"I've got my overalls on and they don't have a pocket. Before you ask, no, you cannot ride on my shoulder like a parrot."

"I never get to have any fun!" He was hanging his head off the edge of the basket and moping.

"Fine. Last time." He perked right up. I murmured 'faker' at him as I lifted him up. Having a unicorn on your shoulder is an experience, let me tell you. Because he has hooves instead of claws, he has to grip my shirt with his teeth to stay on as I walk. He resembles a flower corsage more than a parrot.

As I climbed the stairs I could feel him bouncing around like crazy on my shoulder. "You still OK?"

"Mmmmm mmm." I had to laugh at him. When I was younger it was a fun game to have him ride like this. Now that I'm bigger, he bounces around too much.

I could hear voices coming from the main room as I stepped into the kitchen. By the Gods, I hoped it wasn't another upset member of the town council. Just because I created them doesn't mean they listen to me. Damn squirrels. They listened to me one time. One! Somehow the family figured that out. They are relentless about nagging me to tell them to go somewhere else. Is it my fault the purple squirrels like our town?

The still-room is just off the kitchen. It's original to the house. Initially, it was to be a spring room. Before the first world war, people used them to keep eggs, milk, and other perishables cool. Later, the maids or the cooks would use the rooms to make cleaning products, medicine, preserves, and other household products. Ours was Grandmother's domain. This was where all the magic happened, literally. Grandmother was very well known for her skill in medicinal potions and creams. The still-room was her workshop. I carefully opened the door and stepped inside. The temperature here was at least ten degrees cooler than outside. And that was without a cool spell. With the spell in effect, it was like winter on a blustery day in here. Everything had a proper place inside the room. Toxic herbs were kept in a locked cabinet. Only grandmother and I had a key, and knew the cantrip that would unlock the traps set on it. It's not that we don't trust the family, but too many people have accidents. Poison is permanent.

I heard my name called again. It was time to quit stalling. I quickly stripped off my coveralls and headed for the main room.

Grandmother was sitting in her chair, talking to a sharply dressed man in a black suit. "Grandmother? Did you call for me?"

"Ah, child. Good. Come over here and meet Agent Grimes. He is here to do a basic evaluation of you for the Academy."

Oh, Boy. I stepped over to the chair opposite hers and sat down. "Nice to meet you Agent Grimes."

He smiled at me saying, "Please call me John. Your grandmother has told me quite a bit about you."

I glanced at her and she smiled. I was in so much trouble here. "Hopefully it was all good."

"So far everything checks out. We are looking forward to having you at the Academy next week. It's my understanding that magic teachers are going to be provided?" He looked toward Grandmother.

"That is what the Council keeps telling me. They promised to help train her."

"Good. I just wanted to check on that. This has been my pet project for a few years. Ever since the Mason Killer a few years ago, the Bureau has been in need of a magic user on our side. For some reason no one wants to work with us."

"Um." I looked at Grandmother with wide eyes.

"It's OK, Agatha. You can tell him. He will have to be told eventually."

I looked back at the agent who was staring at us funny. "It's like this, Agent Grimes. Those of us in the Witch and Wizard community dislike and fear the government."

"Why? We have always worked with your councils and have protected you in the courts from the anti-paras groups."

"It was the Purge." The fear was too deeply ingrained in the community's psyche to change our opinion of the Feds.

"That was a century ago. I don't understand." I hoped that the rest of the Feds weren't this clueless.

"In this country, the covens fear any government involvement. Any at all. We are taught in witch school to report things to the head of the coven before calling 911. It's an unwritten rule. Don't involve the government, ever. Too many of us remember what happened the last time we mixed or joined forces. The United States government was not involved, but they knew about it. We know that for sure. One spell. That is all it took to practically eradicate one of the largest species of paranormals on the planet. The fear is genuine and justified."

"Still, it was a century ago. Governments change. Ours is more accountable than those in the past. I don't understand. Don't the covens in Europe work with the governments there? I mean, they were the ones that caused it."

Out of the corner of my eye, I saw Grandmother wince. I let out a breath and tried to correct him. "Forget everything you think you know about what happened after the Purge." I took a deep breath. Witch history was my favorite topic.

"OK. History lesson. The Spell. It was not supposed to kill anyone. That was not its function. The power that was raised and the blood that was spilled was supposed to bind the vampires and shield them from the Germanic covens. No one expected what happened. We are not normally killers. Respect has been a rule that paranormals have lived by until the Purge. The mundane governments, including yours, all patted themselves on the backs that we saved the day and the war could now be fought on even terms. For us, it was as if the sun froze in the sky and the dead rose from the Earth. It was a thing of horror and disdain. Thousands of paranormals died. Tens of thousands. Imagine a city such as Atlanta or Nashville. Now remove all the people from it and kill them. That was how many were killed in the Purge. The amount that survived was minuscule compared to what their population had been."

Agent Grimes had a look of horror upon his face. "But the history books? I don't understand."

"History is written by the victors, Agent Grimes. Remember that." That came from Grandmother.

"Right. Think back to pivotal historic events. The Battle of Hastings, Battle of Bannockburn, Masada, and Caesar's defeat of the Druids on Anglesey. History is filled with battles and executions of the wrong person or thing. It's all a matter of point-of-view. From the Allied governments POV, the vampires died and the war was won. From our POV, it was a monstrous war crime. The leaders of the covens in question stood trial for their crimes. So did those on the German side."

"I have never read that. I know I have never read that."

"That would be because we didn't tell you. Most paranormals know the true history. It is what we are taught so the same mistake doesn't happen again. Something else that we have kept hidden is that the enemy covens were completely destroyed. Gone. Down to the last member and family. None remain today."

"How? Why? That's mass murder!"

"Agent, we didn't do it. No witch or wizard alive today committed that crime. Rumors exist that it was done by the Vampires. However, they refute it too. It is a rare occurrence to see a vampire anywhere in Europe. They avoid it like we do the plague."

I looked over at Grandmother. She nodded to continue. All righty then. "After the war was over and victory was at hand, the magical alliance broke up. The governments of the world promised to help integrate us and we promised to listen to what they had to say. Betrayal is such a dirty word, but that is what happened nonetheless. The public as a whole was scared, and the governments of the world did nothing to help change that. Your agency herded the Weres onto reservations so they could be watched and experimented on. The Fae melted back into their forests and groves. Very few are seen these days. Everyone else played it safe and hid themselves from public view. Then another war loomed. You came to us for help. And what happened?"

"You said no."

"Yes. We as a whole, said no. The covens in Britain cooperated, but they had no choice. Everyone knew where they lived and where their children went to school. Many were taken into protective custody to force compliance. In this country, only the Weres were at risk. They took a chance and told you no. We went the smarter route this time: Newspaper articles, public radio pieces, and show-and-tell. We forced Congress and the White House to meet with us on our terms and we insisted on formal recognition and laws. For you, the Salem Witch Trials were history, but for us it was still happening. In the years between wars, many a small town witch or magical practitioner was burned out of their homes or run out of the town they grew up in. People were scared. Going to the police and asking for protection was like painting a big W on your head and asking for trouble. It was not all that unusual to come home and find white-sheeted men tearing up your yard and burning a cross in it."

He started to speak, but I held up my hand. "We fought your war for you. Once we found out it was a demon incursion we were glad to help. Those things are nothing but trouble to begin with. This time, when the war ended, we did not go back into obscurity. We stayed. We call it being out-of-the-broom-closet. So back to your original question. We still to this day avoid police and any government official. That is what the various councils are for. They talk to you. We don't.."

The agent was nodding his head. "That explains so very much.

I've been beating my head on the table wondering why no one would talk to us. Having a trained magical person on our team would make so much difference. We are literally flying blind sometimes. The Weres help some, but they are mainly muscle. We need magic. We need you."

I chuckled at him. "I'm sorry, Agent Grimes."

"Call me John."

"I'm sorry, John. I don't mean to laugh. But you said you have Weres on your team?"

"We do. Why, is something wrong?"

"Did you ask any of them why we wouldn't work with you?"

He thought for a moment. "I did. I remember asking one of the Bears that very question."

"What did he say?"

"Something to the effect that he could ask his council for direction. Why?"

"The Weres are taught the same history as we are. As I am. They could have told you what I just did. He was asking you if he could ask permission of his council. Only they can approve a history lesson for a mundane. Especially a government one."

"It's a matter of POV again, Agent. You just have to understand us better." My grandmother looked him in the eyes as she spoke. "To answer the unasked question. The answer is yes. The council did give us permission to tell you. You need to understand the dynamic here. The lesser paranormals know this as well as we do. It's all about balance, something our government forgets about. Now, enough history for one day. You are here to speak to Agatha. Please feel free to do so." She stood up from her chair and walked back toward the kitchen.

I listened for the still-room door but failed to hear it.

"Is she always so..."

"Stern. Demanding. Scary. That would be yes, John. She is very sweet to me. I've lived here since I was seven."

"So. The Academy. It's my understanding that you actually want to go. It's not the council pushing you?"

"Yes, it's something I would love to do. I like the idea of police work and helping people."

John looked down at the files in front of him for a moment. "I've read all the files and studied what was available about you. What happened when you were seven? Our basic background check was met with anger and fear beyond what it should be."

I sighed. Everything always comes back to the birthday party from hell. "Everyone from here calls it "The Incident." They are trying to be nice, in their own way. My father was killed on my sixth birthday. Mother very nearly didn't get over it. Her sister, my Aunt Camilla, organized a seventh birthday party for me without telling mother first. It was a surprise. Mother was just starting to come around when suddenly the yard was filled with loud, noisy children, and fussy parents. Uncle Harrison, Camilla's first husband. No, I think he was number two. Three? Her husband. There have been so many. He bought me a Unicorn for my birthday."

"Wait. A Unicorn. Like a live Unicorn? Looks like a horse with a horn sticking out? That Unicorn?"

Mundanes. "Yes, agent. A unicorn. Well-to-do Witches ride them. It's a status thing. So the unicorn shows up. All the other girls scream and want to pet it. The mothers are very jealous and fawn all over Camilla for such a rare gift. Which is what she wanted to happen. My mother barely noticed. She was still recovering and was very quiet that day. Even though it was my party, I didn't want it. I just wanted to sit with my mother and talk. She had been sick for so long and I missed having her aware of me. Camilla could not leave it alone and had to have a spectacle."

"What happened? Your file says you lost control, but not the details."

"My magic is... lopsided. Simple things I can do without any problem." I pointed at his two pens on top of my file. I spoke the word 'lifa.' The two pens grew legs and stood up. Speaking the word 'vig', I had them begin to fight each other. Agent Grimes stared at his pen and pencil set as they began to wrestle each other on the table. I let them fight for a moment and said 'létta.' They went back to being pens and just lay there. The agent carefully picked them up with two fingers and examined them.

"I can start fires, move things, and change my appearance quite easily. It is the larger things that cause issues. Bad or unexpected things can happen. At the party, I yelled at my aunt and uncle. I didn't want a unicorn. I wanted a pony. I wanted one more than a stupid unicorn." A muffled cry could be heard for a moment.

The agent looked around puzzled. "Did you hear that?"

I ignored his question and tried to finish the stupid story. "I screamed and cried and demanded they take the unicorn away and just bring me a pony. Camilla and Harrison refused and began to argue with me over it. Remember, I was seven years old. So, I turned and zapped it. To this day I couldn't tell you what spell I used. I truly think I made one up. There was a bright flash of light and the unicorn began talking! He was not just talking, he was cursing. Cursing me and everyone else he found. Parents freaked out, the kids all screamed and cried, and my mother fainted dead away. Camilla started to yell at me as she checked on mother. She was berating me for being such a terrible daughter. I was so upset I turned to the talking unicorn and zapped him again trying to fix it. At the time I had zero formal training. Both magic surges were off-the-cuff, which is highly dangerous for the unwary."

"What happened? Did you fix it?"

Reaching into my pocket I pulled out Fergus. "What am I, some kind of show-and-tell experiment now?" The unicorn looked at the agent. "What are you looking at? Never seen a micro unicorn before?"

"That would be no," I said with a smile. "John, I created Fergus here. He acts as my familiar. One of these days, I just know I will remember what I did and change him back to normal. He stays with me just in case that happens."

"That's one of the reasons. The other involves a freaking huge ass cat that thinks I'm a chew toy!" The unicorn freaked himself out and began looking for Zeus.

"But you still have magic right?"

"Oh, yeah. The council thought Fergus was humorous. They liked the squirrels too."

"Those I have seen." He was watching Fergus move around, not totally believing in unicorns. "Can you control it, the bad magic?"

"Sort of. I try not to do large spells or make up stuff. For the most part nothing happens. I've only zapped inanimate objects lately. So, my control is improving some."

"Well, overpowered or not, we both want and need you. Would you like to go to the Academy this week? I have to ask."

"Yes! If you will still take me."

He stood up and picked up his files and pen set. I expect that the set might wind up in the trash. Mundanes can be funny that way. "Your grandmother has the admissions packet. Registration and classes start next weekend. We have a dorm room with your name on it. There is a pool for room registration, so I don't know who or what you might get as a roommate."

"Cool! I've never shared a room before. Well, except for Fergus."

"Great. We look forward to seeing you." Agent Grimes took one last look around the room and went out the front door. There was a big black Suburban sitting in the rotunda driveway. I watched him leave, then went in search of Grandmother. We had a lot of planning to do.

CHAPTER THREE

PACKING WAS EASY. The FBI was going to supply all my clothing and basic personal needs. All I needed to bring was what they called personal items. No outside electronics were allowed. According to the information Agent Grimes left, I was allowed to bring spell components and necessary "witch stuff". Both grandmother and I got a huge laugh at that. I actually said, "Witch stuff!" We struggled over what to bring and what would fit in my small suitcases. Finally, fed up with the whole process, grandmother called someone. She somehow obtained approval for me to bring whatever and as much as I needed or wanted. The FBI had never had a real Witch recruit before. It was as much a learning experience for them as for me. I hoped they had good insurance. Because shit just got real!

"Did you pack my stall? How about my feeding trough?" Stupid of me to think the car ride would be fun. Fergus had spent the first hour complaining. Now he had moved on to what I'd packed.

"You watched me pack your stuff, Fergus. Chill out! Grandmother gave us money. I can buy you a replacement if we forgot something. I doubt that is even possible, since it feels like we have the entire house following us." I glanced over my shoulder at the panel truck following us. I would be learning to control my magic, so I would need various supplies. Grandmother insisted that I bring everything. She actually convinced the FBI to give me a portion of both a greenhouse and one of their labs for all the stuff. We grew all our own spell components. Grandmother didn't trust the prepackaged stuff. If she didn't like it, neither did I. "Trust your instincts" is one of her mantras.

I was originally supposed to fly, but Grandmother suggested I travel with the truck. Much of what we packed was extremely valuable and hard to find. Losing it from mishandling or theft would not aid me in my studies. The trip was longer, but for someone who rarely left the boundaries of Blackbriar Heights, it was marvelous. I was constantly pointing out landmarks and mundane stuff like farm tractors and tractor trailers. Our town was tiny, compared to many of the cities we passed through. The highway system in our part of Maine had not been updated in over half a century. It wasn't so much that the highway department didn't care, but due primarily to Agnes Pickleberry. Or as we called her, Ol' Picklebucket. She was one of the town elders who lived right on the edge of our boundary. Every time the highway department brought in machines to do the work, she would hex them. She was our town bard and absolutely hated loud noise. Inasmuch as she was on the town council, no one could stop her. She led the State to believe we had upgraded roads when we didn't.

Setting wards was one skill I could do without setting myself on fire or something. The first night we stopped at a roadside motel. The FBI agents who were escorting me and the truck looked at me funny when I set the wards. I tried to explain what I was doing, but it was like talking to one of the purple squirrels. Dumb as a post. If this is what they had to work with, I could see the need for paranormals in the service. More brawn than brain. Squatting near the truck, I lit a candle with my finger. Speaking quickly, I laid out the basic boundaries surrounding the car, truck, and our rooms. Anyone who attempted to break in would be frozen as if in amber until I released them. It was a very effective spell. Grandmother used it every fruit picking season. Back in Blackbriar, it was a right-of-passage to avoid her traps and bring back an apple. I stood and set my cantrips with the word 'reiði.' The agents looked at me as I walked back.

"Everything OK, Miss?"

"Yes Agent Carlson, everything is just fine. I set a ward on the truck, the car, and our rooms. If anyone other than the four of us tampers with them, they will be trapped until morning."

He squinted and looked down at me. "Trapped how?"

"Have you ever gotten rubber cement on your fingers? Imagine swimming in it. That is what any thief will experience. They won't be harmed unless they attack me. That I don't recommend."

"Oh. Sorry. We don't have much experience with witch stuff. There are exactly two wizards on the payroll, but they only work on the really high-profile cases."

That surprised me. "Really? I was told you didn't have anyone on staff."

"Well, they are private contractors of a sort. We have to pay them to help us. They are Russian."

That made more sense to me. Ever since the Demon War, Russian practitioners worked mostly freelance. The Slavic covens paid a heavy price to defeat the Demon hordes. Only an idiot would raise a Demon, much less a Demon Prince. That was exactly what the Thule Society did. There are reasons why most practitioners of High Magick are old guys. They study for years to just learn how to make the perfect circle. The slightest mistake, a wrong letter or a hash mark in the wrong place can spell disaster. Even a pronunciation mistake can cause an incursion of things best left alone. Grandmother taught me the basics and made me promise to never, ever, use the knowledge without proper supervision. Demonic possession is not something you want to happen to you. Putting the genie back in the proverbial bottle required a great deal of power. The Russian Volkhvy supplied that power. They sacrificed themselves to hold the demons at bay so the Allies could take care of a demon possessed

Madman in the heart of Berlin. The Russian paranormals have not been the same since.

"I understand. Thank you. I doubt anyone will touch the truck, but if they do, tomorrow should be fun! Good night."

As I crawled into bed I giggled to myself. This was going to be so much fun. The FBI really had no idea what was in store for them.

I got very little sleep that night. It may have been the strange bed, the musty room, the complaining Unicorn, or the banging on my door at the crack of dawn.

Throwing on a robe, I blinked a few times to wake up. I could hear a loud commotion outside my door. Flashing red and blue lights showed through the curtains covering my windows. The knocking started again. I opened the door to find Agent Carlson in mid-knock. "Is there something wrong Agent?"

"We didn't believe you, but someone tried to break into the truck last night!"

I giggled. "Really?"

"Yes, Ma'am. We have three on the rear door and one in the front. The local law enforcement is bitching up a storm. One of their guys got stuck too."

It really wasn't funny, but I chuckled to myself. "Let me get dressed and I will release them. Tell the locals they are fine. It's a non-lethal spell. I'll be just a moment." I stepped back into my room and began pulling out clothing.

"What's wrong? Is this flea trap on fire?"

"Nope. Someone tripped the wards. Including the local police."

Fergus was still laughing when we stepped back outside. Dawn was only a few minutes away as the first rays of sunlight worked their way over the tree line. In the early morning light, it was easy to see the three men caught in the act of prying the door open. With my escort agents following, I slowly walked around the truck. The man attempting to break the glass to get in the truck cab was wearing a sheriff's uniform. I pointed that out to Carlson.

"Hey! Is that her?"

26

Another man in a sheriff's uniform approached me. His face was red and inflamed. "See here, you. How dare you bring your witch bitch into my county and trap my man in your evil spells!" He reached out and tried to grab me. Carlson and the other agent were not fast enough to prevent him from grabbing my arm. Immediately, my protections kicked in.and he was thrown ten feet from me. My two agents just turned and stared at me. "A word to the wise gentlemen. Never grab a practitioner with violence on your mind. It does not end well. I might suggest you call in some reinforcements? This will get messy, now."

They thought that was good advice and called in the Connecticut State Police. The Sheriff was arrested and so were the four thieves. It seems there was a rash of robberies along this stretch of highway that had been going unsolved for years. Local law enforcement was always unable to find any of the culprits. The Sheriff had a heck of a little business going on. Carlson and his team were credited with the capture and arrest.

"Miss, I wish you would reconsider."

"Agent Carlson. I am not even a rookie yet. Hell, I haven't spent one night at Quantico yet. You and your boys can have all the credit. There will be plenty more arrests to go around. Trust me."

After that, the Agents were much nicer to me. We had no other major problems until we hit Interstate 95. Then I got to experience the true meaning of a traffic jam. The agents pointed out the many features of Quantico as we entered the base. The Marines wanted to search the truck, but my agents produced paperwork forbidding that. Grandmother had keyed some of what was in the truck for me alone. It made me cringe to think of what would happen if someone else grabbed it. Instead of heading to the dorms, I had them take me to the greenhouse first, then whatever Lab I would be using. I needed to get that truck unloaded. Too many breakable things around here for my tastes. The lab was actually part of the greenhouse. Bonus, as Fergus would say. That unicorn has spent entirely too much time watching TV.

The lab and greenhouse were located on the edge of the Marine area. It was away from the residential areas and downwind of any school or civilian area. It made me wonder what was here before me. I investigated the building before I unloaded anything. The green-house needed a bit of work, but it would do nicely.

"Agents, I need for you to step back. This spell should work, but sometimes strange things happen when I cast." I focused on the rear of the truck. Using my finger, I lit a candle and concentrated on the flame. Picturing what I wished to happen, I spoke my words of power: 'atrið, bera, and dúði.' I opened my eyes just as the door opened on its own and boxes began to float out of the truck. Pointing at the small attached warehouse, the door rolled up. The floating boxes began stacking themselves in the order that I visualized. The last part of the truck was filled with herbs and other growing things. I waved my hands with a wrist twist worthy of ZZ-Top, and directed them toward the greenhouse. When the last crate left the truck, the door rolled down and locked on its own accord. I glanced behind me. All three agents just stood with their mouths open at the specta-cle. Setting the ward took three times longer than usual. There were too many kinds of people on this base. I had to ward against everyone both friend and foe. Until I had time to lock up some of the spell components, there was a great risk of accidental poisoning or death.

It was midday by the time I finished. We said goodbye to the truck driver. They said his name was Marcus. That left me with Agent Carlson and Agent Stevenson. The two of them drove me over to my assigned dormitory. It was time for my adventure to begin. The agents supplied me with maps and my small traveling case. I hugged both of them.

"Agents, thank you for everything. That was a very interesting trip."

"Ma'am, we will look you up when you get to Rookie status. Maybe you can teach us a thing or two."

I smiled at them. "That I will do, Agent."

Before I could speak the name Carlson, he said, "Bob." The other agent called himself Bill.

"Thank you, Bob and Bill. I think I can handle it from here on out."

Giving them no second thought, I climbed the stairs into the admissions building. A large desk occupied the central lobby. I watched as various agents ran to and fro in the hallways beyond the lobby. A blond woman sat behind the desk, checking off names and yelling directions to people who were obviously students.

"Name?"

I was still staring at her when what she said registered in my brain. "I'm sorry. Were you speaking to me?"

She narrowed her eyes. "I said, 'Name?'" She sounded like a real bitch. Trust me, I know the breed. Half my family could give her lessons. I choose to live my life following the words of the prophet James Dalton. "Be nice. Until it's time to not be nice." Words to live by.

"Agatha Blackmore." Her eyes widened, and she pressed a button on her desk. There was a loud humming and clear Plexiglas screens descended from the ceiling, enclosing both the desk and me.

I looked at the box that I was in and smiled. "Is there a reason for this?" I pointed at the walls. The woman behind the desk flinched when I raised my hands. Agents came running from doors located along the walls.

"Isn't this a little much for new student orientation?" I smiled at the woman. It was almost time to not be nice.

"I have my orders! Cover her!" She pointed the agents at me.

"What do you think Fergus?" Asking the Unicorn for advice is probably never a good idea but what the hell.

"Show them what you can do. It's not like they can hurt you. Besides, *they* recruited *you*."

He had a point. Strange when he made sense. "I'm new here, but I don't think this is how I am supposed to be greeted. Can anyone call Agent John Grimes or his boss and tell them I'm here?"

The agents all held weapons on me while the bitchy blond franti-cally called for help on her phone. I shook my head. Time to go. "I'm leaving. Anyone want to drive me back to Maine?" Of course, no one answered me. I waved my hand and spoke a word of power, 'skera.' The three-inch-thick plexiglass walls cracked and shattered into a fine dust. I brushed my clothing off as well as I could. That sort of dust just gets everywhere. I spoke another spell, 'skjald-borg,' and stepped out of the ring of dust. The door to outside was about fifty-feet behind me. I turned and walked toward it. The agents opened fire at that point. The bullets ricocheted off me and began zinging and pinging around the room. I said 'stǫðva' and made a stop motion with my hands. The glass doors to outside shattered as bullets hit them. I continued walking, carefully stepping over the piles of broken glass. Outside on the sidewalk were two Marine Humvees with M240 machine guns mounted on them.

"Halt! On the ground! Get on the ground now!" When is it going to end?

"Seriously? If this is how you treat new students, I'd hate to see what you do to graduating ones." I motioned with my hands, making a breast stroke motion. Both vehicles scraped sideways across the concrete. The gunners on top began to fire at me.

With steel-jacketed rounds bouncing off my shield I sat down on a bench. "You people are really starting to piss me off!" I thought about the spells I knew. I was just about to bring the building down on top of them when a supervisor, accompanied by John Grimes, finally arrived.

"Hi John. Do these belong to you? If they do, you can take me right back to Maine." I pointed at the two now upside-down Humvees and the dozen or so agents pointing guns at me.

"Guns down! Goddammit, put your guns down!" The Agents all put their guns down as ordered.

"Grimes! What in all that's holy is going on here! We have reports of Agents down and buildings under attack echoing all the way to Washington! Who's attacking?" The other man shouted.

I looked at the big handsome agent. "Is he your boss?" John nodded at me. I glared at him. "They attacked me first! If this is how you treat students here I want to go back to Maine!"

"Young lady, I don't know who you think you are, but I was talking to Agent Grimes, not you! So butt out!"

That's it. "Now it's time to not be nice anymore." I waved my hand at the boss and he found himself upside down ten feet in the air. All the agents pointing guns at me joined him.

"So, John. Do I get my ride back to Maine or do I pull that nice building down on top of the mean lady and the men that shot at me?"

John sat down on the bench next to me and put his hands over his face with a groan.

It took several hours to clean up the mess. Flipping the Humvees was just a flick of the wrist. They almost shot at me again. I was starting to see first-hand why no one volunteered to join the Academy. The Witch Council had all but drafted me for this position and they knew it.

"Agatha, please don't leave. We need you badly."

"Yes, I can see that. If this is how you apprehend paranormals who break the law, I'm surprised we even still have a country. All I did was give my name. Why?"

He sighed and rubbed his head some more. If he keeps doing that he won't have any hair left. "My boss, the Director. That would be the guy you made pee his pants by waving him like a flag ten feet in the air. My boss sent word to his assistant. You were coming, and they needed to be aware you were a witch. You were to be given every courtesy and offered your choice in rooms. The assistant passed the message on to the Administration group. They assign rooms and monitor students. Their message said student witch coming, be prepared. They passed the message off to the main desk that said to be on the lookout. A witch is coming, be prepared. So, when you gave your name, it identified you as a witch and all hell broke loose."

"That is the stupidest reason I have ever heard. If you had done this to Grandmother, you might not have a building or even a Marine base any longer. You need to tell them. Hell, have them watch the video from this little adventure. Don't piss off a witch!"

"I know. I'm sorry. Will you stay?"

"You know I have nowhere else to go. Promise me that when the council visits for my training they will not be treated like this?"

Everyone apologized to me. Even piss boy, the director. I finally got my packet for new students and was given directions to the dorm. John drove me there himself. I insisted that he drop me off and not come in. I entered the dorm. Dozens of students were standing around talking. From the pieces of their conversations that I overheard, they were discussing the attack earlier. None of them seemed to have the real story. The lobby had a large TV room and a snack bar. Next to the bar was a small office. I approached the window.

I smiled at the attendant. "I'm here for my room assignment?"

"Name?"

"Agatha Blackmore."

The attendant's eyes got really big and he began to shake. He handed me a key and pointed toward the left. "Second floor, room 242." I guess my name preceded me.

The building had both a stairway and an elevator. I took the stairs. The second floor was a long hall with bathrooms at either end. Great, communal showers. Just like camp. Not that I ever went to camp.

I found my room number and tried the key. The door opened to a medium sized room with two couches, one on either side, and two desks. There was a small wash basin with running water. A small dresser and clothing rack for hangers completed the set. A smallish girl sat on one of the couches.

"Hello."

"Hi there! You must be my new roommate!"

I smiled. "I am. Agatha Blackmore."

"Hi Agatha, I'm Catherine Moore. But you can call me Cat."

From my pocket I heard a voice. "Why do I smell cats?"

I tried to ignore him, but he kept talking. "Agatha, I swear it smells like cat in here. Where have we ended up? The pound?"

My new roommate was looking at me funny. Sighing, I reached into my pocket and set Fergus on the desk.

Cat's eyes widened and she almost purred. She looked at me and said. "Witch?"

Noticing a few things, I smiled. "Werecat?"

She began to laugh, and I joined in. Fergus ignored both of us and paced along the top of the desk. "I swear there has been a cat in here! We need to find it and get rid of it! Damn sneaky cats."

Cat and I looked at each other again and snickered. It was going to be a hell of a year.

CONJURING QUANTICO

How do you cope with magic that goes its own way?

As a second year FBI academy witch, Agatha Blackmore has a certain reputation. After nearly blowing up the school, an untended mid-air incident involving the FBI Director, and declaring war with the US Marines, she has to wonder if she will even see graduation.

But when a rash of mysterious disappearances catches the attention of local authorities Agatha finds herself asked to lend a hand to the investigation. Determined to offer protection where it is needed the most, Agatha and her quirky roommate Cat along with her mini-unicorn familiar Fergus, attempt to unravel the mysteries of the four distinctly magical disappearances before time runs out.

Does Agatha have what it takes to be an agent? Or will everyone that crosses her end up eating chicken feed for the rest of their lives?

Conjuring Quantico (My Book) is the first book in a brand new Urban Fantasy by T. S. Paul.

As a direct sequel to Born a Witch... Drafted by the FBI, T. S. Paul returns with the first book of the Federal Witch Series!

The Federal Witch

Born a Witch Drafted by the FBI! - Now Available in Audio!

Conjuring Quantico - Now Available in Audio!

Magical Probi - Now Available in Audio!

Special Agent in Charge - Now Available in Audio!

Witness Enchantment

Path to Otherwhere

Night of the Unicorn

Invisible Elder

Blood on the Moon

Child of Darkness

A Draft of Dragons - TBD

Cat's Night Out, Tails from the Federal Witch - Audio Available

Serpent Con

Darkness Revealed

Unicorns Are Short

The Standard of Honor

Shade of Honor

Coven Codex

Familiar Magic

Familiar Shadows

Familiar Trials - Fledgling

Familiar Travels

The Wild Hunt

Witching Hour

The Wild Hunt

Furious Magic

The Mongo Files

The Case of the Jamaican Karma -TBD

The Case of the Lazy Magnolia - TBD

The Case of the Rugrat Exorcist -TBD

Monster Hunter

Jack Dalton Book 1

Jack Dalton Book 2

Jack Dalton Book 3

Jack Dalton Book 4

Jack Dalton Book 5

Jack Dalton Book 6

Magical Division Origins

Jack Dalton, Monster Hunter Box Set (1-3)

Jack Dalton, Monster Hunter Box Set (4-6)

Cookbooks From the Federal Witch Universe

Marcella's Garden Cookbook

Fergus Favorites Cookbook

Marcella's Summer Bounty Cookbook

Marcella's Autumn Harvest

Eat and Read Cookbooks

Badger Hole Bar Food Cookbook

Taking it on the Road

Athena Lee Chronicles

The Forgotten Engineer

Engineering Murder

Ghost Ships of Terra

Revolutionary

Insurrection

Imperial Subversion

The Martian Inheritance - Audio Now Available

Infiltration

Prelude to War

War to the Knife

Ghosts of Noodlemass Past

Forgotten Hope

Athena Lee Universe

Shades of Learning

Space Cadets - Coming Soon

Smuggle Life

Double Cross

Politics Equals Death

Cut and Run

A Grand Affair

Short Story Collections

Wilson's War

A Colony of CATTs

Unicorns are Short

Borscht is Boring

Box Sets

The Federal Witch: The Collected Works, Book 1

Chronicles of Athena Lee Book 1-3

Chronicles of Athena Lee Book 4-6

Chronicles of Athena Lee Book 7-9 plus the prequel

Athena Lee Chronicles (10 Book Series)

Standalone or tie-ins

The Tide: The Multiverse Wave

The Lost Pilot

Uncommon Life

Dead in Space

Kutherian Gambit

Alpha Class. The Etheric Academy book 1

Alpha Class - Engineering. The Etheric Academy Book 2

The Etheric Academy (2 Book Series)

Holiday Tales

Watch Where You Dig

Night of the Living Turkeys

Reindeer Don't Fly

Anthologies

Phoenix Galactic

Cupid's Bow

Mysterious Hearts

Journal with a View: July - August - September

Haunted Hearts

Snapshots of Life I

Prime Peek I

Silent Thanks

Non-Fiction

Get that Sh@t off your Cover!: The so-called Miracle Man speaks out

Study Guide and Timeline: The Athena Lee Chronicles

CPSIA information can be obtained
at www.ICGtesting.com
Printed in the USA
LVHW051458280219
609070LV00019B/953